The Fairy Tale Book
OF BIFFORD C. WELLINGTON

by T. A. Young

illustrated by
theodore gallmeyer

138 IN PROGRESS PUBLISHING
NEW YORK

138 In Progress Publishing
Dover Plains, New York
www.138inprogresspublishing.com

Edited by Marian Grudko

Library of Congress Control Number: 2015919199
ISBN: 978-0-9982768-3-0

Printed in the United States of America
First Edition: June 2017

The Literary Pantheon Speaks about

The Fairy Tale Book
OF BIFFORD C. WELLINGTON

*"I must confess these tales easily surpass
the originals. Brilliant."*
— JACOB GRIMM

*"I imagine myself sitting across from
Wellington, discussing these stories until
a slot machine opens up."*
— H.C. ANDERSON

*"Be careful, Wellington.
They banished me for less."*
— PUBLIUS OVIDIUS NASO

"Knocked me out of my shoe."
— CINDERELLA

"Dazzling! I feel sleep-deprived."
— SCHEHERAZADE

*"If I catch that plagiarizing toad
anywhere near my office,
I'm going to kill him."*
— MOTHER GOOSE

*"These stories. True? Not true?
Eh! Does it even matter?
Only that the matter is in the matter.
And I have no idea
what I mean by that."*
— PICO KAFKA
(author of The Trinity of Stooges)

*"I'm not one to exaggerate, so when
I tell you this collection is astonishing,
the grandest achievement of mankind,
a colossus that makes the Pillars of
Hercules look like a couple of chipped
Legos, you can trust me."*
— FRANÇOIS RABELAIS

For Sweetie, Muppit and Maximus

Dragons will wander about the waste places, and the phoenix will soar from her nest of fire into the air. We shall lay our hands upon the basilisk, and see the jewel in the toad's head. Champing his gilded oats, the Hippogriff will stand in our stalls, and over our heads will float the Blue Bird singing of beautiful and impossible things, of things that are lovely and that never happen, of things that are not and that should be. But before this comes to pass we must cultivate the lost art of Lying.

— OSCAR WILDE,
"THE DECAY OF LYING"

The Fairy Tale Book
OF BIFFORD C. WELLINGTON

Table of Contents

Preface

"Daye Six. We are well in it now. The sun can only suggest itself through the heavy canopy. And yet, our vision! We see all things at once. From whence this unearthly light?"

(From Thee Journalle Recordyng thee Travells of M. Winch Clofftrede, ca. 1346, early explorer of the Magical Forest)

Once upon a time I was in my basement and I saw, lying beneath the hot-water heater, a very small, very dead mouse. He - or she, (I'm not a mouse-ologist) - was barely an inch long, not including his tail. (I know: "How can you exclude the tail?")

Being an animist and believing that nature is happiest with nature, I took the mouse outside and placed him on a pile of damp leaves where I hoped he best belonged under the circumstances. I covered him with a few leaves and said, "I'm sorry you're dead." I felt pretty bad, but found some solace in my "return to nature" theory. I'll take little solace over no solace ten times out of ten. That's called hope. The end.

I would like to believe that the above story is the kind told by the denizens of the magical forest, not because I'm in it, but because it's a tale that may have meaning to its audience; or they'd find it touching or amusing. Or crazy.

Luckily, they have better stories for us than we have for them.

My cousin Mintsy - short for Mintsford - came back from Germany a month ago and recounted to us a journey he took into the legendary Black Forest. He brought back some interesting artifacts from that trek, among them, a magic pebble, a magic twig, a magic leaf, and a magic parking ticket. Though the magic was not demonstrable, it was palpable, which is even better for those of us who, when it comes to what really matters, prefer faith to proof. Mintsy heard many stories from the local traders, merchants, peddlers of maps, amulets, charms, wands and wishing caps, purveyors of Priceless Lessons and Equivocal Luck, and he recorded them to share upon his return.

Stories earn their truth; time is their test. So it makes sense that the Land of The Magical Forest endures, made timeless by the truths that abide within. Its Truths are not so much time-less as time-impervious.

Here, we share stories full of what we would call tiny miracles - or magic, if you will. Perhaps you will look up from its pages and say, "Son of a gun, these two worlds are not so different. The forest does not have all the magic; there is some here, too. And so close to the mall. Imagine that." We would be quite happy if that were to happen.

Let us know.
—BCW

One final note: I have another cousin, Donavan Magpie Chillpass. He wanted you to know.

The Dragon and The Blue Elf;
Or, Seeking Pigeons,
One Sometimes Finds
Dragons

Once upon a time
there was a
dragon
whose scales
of emeralds and
sapphires and
rubies and
gold shone

so brightly they hurt the eyes.
When the dragon moved it was like the
shimmying of suns and the waltz of gal-

axies. His body wound around lakes and mountains in circles and half circles for miles and miles, rising and falling with his breathing, expanding and receding like a bejeweled ocean. Mortals would confuse him for the horizon at midnight or the aurora borealis or Phoebe's diadem.

And to think he had once been the yolk of an egg barely the size of Leda, Jupiter's smallest moon. How the little ones grow!

You would be surprised by how many could never see the dragon. So oblivious were some that they would walk right through him as if he were no more than a gust of vivifying air.

Then there was the blue elf, so labeled for his form and hue. He, too, could suffer from invisibility, though he could not be walked through. And he was very, very small.

This elf was a collector of the residue of wasted motions and of exclamation points. He would use the latter to build delicate towers of scarcely more than two dimensions that would rise to great heights, then tumble back to earth like a billion black toothpicks vibrating and spinning like quarks: up and down, top and bottom, strange and charmed. The former he stuck in mason jars. (Funny how the parenthetical stuff can end up being important later on, but not always.)

On one day dedicated to this avocation, the elf drove his wagon - pulled by a badger and a mole, the mole banging into the badger every second step, the badger lurching along, making up in focus for what he lacked in grace - west.

The elf had heard that there was a convention of pigeons in from New York and knew those neurotic birds would provide a plethora of precious punctuation.

Instead, he ran into the dragon.

The elf rarely spoke to the dragon for the obvious reason: he was a poor source of exclamation points. One would think that the wisdom of the dragon, being axiomatic, would make up for the lack of desired marks. But you know elves: it's all about the punctuation.

He dismounted from his wagon and strolled over to the dragon. On this day he let himself walk right into him. Literally. He stopped between the curved wall behind him and the curved wall before him, awed by the encircling universe.

The dragon - whose patience was as axiomatic as his wisdom (there was a Buddhist squirrel who knew that these two were the same) - waited for the elf to reappear. As he waited, he pondered into existence four galaxies, seven billion stars, countless planets, and one new species of flower.

Out came the elf. Beyond the enchanted forest it was a Saturday.

As soon as he was able to reorient himself, he walked over to the dragon's head.

"That was something," said the elf.

The dragon nodded. The elf thought about the pointlessness of having brought his exclamation-point-collecting-sack.

"Who's responsible for all that stuff? You? What's the point of creating all that if we just walk through it? Why do you let us? Can't you make us see? Can you make yourself impermeable? Do you just fade in and out? What kind of existence is that?"

"It's a shame," said the dragon, "that I don't collect question marks."

"For an individual of your stature, you don't exactly chase the big picture."

"What is the big picture?"

"All this!" said the elf, spreading his arms to indicate the length of the dragon, which was pretty ironic, considering the span of an elf's outstretched arms.

"How much does that gesture encompass?"

The blue elf attempted a suitable reply, but what came out was something that sounded like, "Ack." (How eloquent the articulations of futility.) He had grokked that soon he would ride away, looking at the backsides of a blind mole and a clumsy badger as they drew him through the woods to his home. He realized that the mole was meant to be blind and the badger was meant to be clumsy and that he - the blue elf - was fulfilling his destiny to be blue and an elf, and the dragon was just being what he was and that it was a terrible thought, no, a wonderful thought, no, he was right the first time, it was a terrible thought that things just are.

A few days later - it was Wednesday beyond the enchanted forest - as he was working on his tower of exclamation points, there was knock on his door. Down went the tower; the elf went to the door. There was the dragon.

"I'd invite you in…."

"You have great humor," noted the dragon.

"I came to answer your questions. I will leave nothing out. But I promise you that even after I tell you all this, you will remain unsatisfied."

The elf paused, then said resignedly, "Then you know what? Forget it. I'll be fine. I'll tell you why: just knowing you're around is good enough for me. I'm not kidding."

As he turned away, the dragon said, "Elf, you may want to consider loosening the lids on those mason jars. Consider all the passion they contain. They may be needed."

Here we pause for an ambiguous sigh. (A blue jay who heard the sigh thought it was "Om," but she was probably just reading into things.)

So the blue elf was content with simply knowing that the truth was out there and everything seemed to be under control and, really, there was no need to know what the hell was going on in the grand scheme of things.

The funny thing is the mole had told him pretty much the same thing. But who listens to a mole?

The Gentle Lad and The Gryphon

Once there was a gentle lad who spent his days moving the cows from here to there, the goats from there to here, the pigs and chickens and dogs and horses from this place to that. The days were long and busy, but he didn't mind. The animals were always pleasant and cooperative, moving in the right direction even before he would start shooing or waving or whistling to get them there.

When the work was finished, the gentle lad would go for walks in the enchanted forest adjacent to his family's farm. Because the farm had been there for many generations, the denizens of this forest had watched its people prosper and suffer and prosper again, and had grown comfortable with their closeness. Never did either side feel uncomfortable with the other, even on those occasions when an elf, pixie or drag-on-kid would stroll or stray into the apple orchard or strawberry patch.

For this reason the gentle lad was always welcome in the forest. He had more friends who were badgers, buzzards and basilisks than he had the human kind.

Often, the gentle lad would wander into the forest and close his eyes. This was part of a game he played with the creatures. When they saw him stop, one of them would take his hand and lead him deep into the woods; his eyes would remain shut until they stopped. He was never disappointed when he opened them: serious bubbles, flying flowers, picnicking sprites, dubious unicorns, singing rocks, promising rainbows, wa-terfalls, rivers, autumn.

This time it was a wolf that guided him.

He opened his eyes to the wonder of wonders: sitting proudly in the shadow of a black mountain, a gryphon as big and as noble as the stone Sphinx in the mythical land called Egypt. By comparison, the manticore - whose body was that of an enormous lion - was a poppy seed. Each of the black talons of the gryphon was larger than the oxen that pulled the plow. Each barb that extended from a feather's shaft was an arrow of steel. To liken its head to that of a bird or its hind parts to those of a lion would be like comparing a hummingbird's beak to the armored prow of a

Viking warship.

His eyes were twin Jupiters.

A hawk perched on the gryphon's shoulder.

The gryphon lowered itself to look at the gentle lad. "You are a boy. Where is your magic?"

"I have none, I think."

"Then what are you doing here?"

"I often visit the forest. I have many friends here."

The hawk turned

towards the gryphon and spoke into his ear.

"What you say is true. You are liked and trusted here. You are a rare animal."

"You are, too, I think."

"There are four of us. All of the same litter. Not hatched as some think. Born."

"How old are you?"

"We are from the time of giants so great they could pull down the moon, polish it and place it back in the sky; giants who had two arms or two hundred arms; giants who were the sentinels of the gods. It was a giant who out of drunkenness and hunger, ate one of your moons. It was a giant whose anger caused him to stomp so hard, he tilted the earth to one side. And another giant's anger that made him exhale so powerfully, the wind blew the heavens farther from this planet than the gods had intended. This was before the age of man. This world was larger then."

"That's old."

"You have a lifespan three-thousand times that of a mouse. Is that old?"

"To a mouse, I suppose."

"To a gryphon, you are a mayfly. Were you to live a thousand of your lifetimes, you would not live one of my days. To some, I am the mayfly."

The gentle lad felt weak. His world had changed. The wolf that was his guide sat beside him. The lad had never considered himself either great or small; in fact, he never considered himself at all. His happiness came from the worlds around him, the magical and the mundane. Now he was not only a something, he was an insignificant something in the scheme of things.

"You are a sad creature," said the lad.

"I am strong but unchallenged. I am a guardian with nothing to guard. One should not outlast his world. One should not outlive one's purpose."

The lad and the gryphon sat silently for some time, deep in thought. The hawk and the wolf, too, sat patiently until the wolf felt obliged to nuzzle the boy; it was time to return home. The boy rose and felt it appropriate to bow to the gryphon. "Will you be here tomorrow?"

The gryphon responded by spreading his wings, creating a storm of wind and thunder and lightning, causing animals to cower and scramble, turning land and air and sea dark as night. The world seemed to howl. Then day returned.

"I must stretch my wings, but I shall return. Perhaps we shall speak again, lad. You are an interesting creature: you change. The way you see, I mean. You are not the same creature I met just moments ago. You must tell me how you do this. And why."

And with that, the earth shook, and he was gone.

The gentle lad never ceased to be gentle. The gryphon remained a gryphon. They did meet again, when the lad was no longer a lad, but close to the end of his life. The gryphon was unchanged.

"Your time is ending," said the gryphon.

"There is still time for me, I think. You have been gone long."

"Mere seconds. Mere seconds. The creatures of your world are so fragile, what a second can do to you."

"I think I see your sadness, now. My kind passes so quickly; you endure eternities. But our happiness….perhaps we are both allotted the same amount of happiness, no matter the time we have to feel it. My kind has to fit our happiness into much less time and do not seem terribly efficient about it. How we do waste what we have. Are gryphons any better at it?"

"We shall see." The gryphon did an odd thing: he pecked once at his own breast, and a trickle of blood appeared. He then lowered himself almost to the ground.

"Put your hand on the cut I have made." The gentle old man did so. The gryphon raised himself.

"We shall see if you have enough happiness left for all your remaining days," said the gryphon.

"I need little," said the gentle old man; and the gryphon knew this as truth.

"We shall see. It is a test of time. What an interesting test this will be."

The gentle man had no idea that he had been turned into a young lad again until he had reached his home.

And this is how the gentle lad and the gryphon became very old friends. Very old.

The Wasp and
The Butterfly

Once upon a time a wasp and a butterfly were heading towards the same flower from opposite directions. Creatures who don't understand wasps and butterflies would have assumed they were both flying under the influence judging from the way they bounced and spiraled toward their target. But that is wrong: they were both sober and both meant business. As a result of the difference in distance from their respective starting points, their different speeds, and the wind, they arrived at the flower at the same time. (Destiny!)

They glared at each other. Again, one who does not understand these creatures would assume the wasp had the advantage what with his stinger and all. But you can't underestimate butterflies.

Oh, it wasn't pretty. They batted and pushed and swatted, pouncing on each other without mercy. Fortunately, their weight prevented them from doing any real harm to each other.

But they were irritating the hell out of the flower.

She - a pretty little dandelion named Juniper (from her father's side of the family) - felt her turf getting torn up from all the crashing and scraping on her delicate corolla. When she had had enough, Juniper mustered her strength and clapped her petals together.

The wasp and the butterfly fell to the earth, stunned.

Neither was hurt too badly and they were able to hobble, then to hop and then to fly away.

Because they lived in a very big field, they never met up again. But the teensy little scars and the enormous emotional residue resulting from that raging battle became the stuff of legend. The narratives of their savage exchange - in the hands of the bards, minstrels, and poets - countless and varied and contradictory - would mold the hearts and minds of generations of wasps and butterflies who would recount the godlike contest of their respective ancestors in their respective epics.

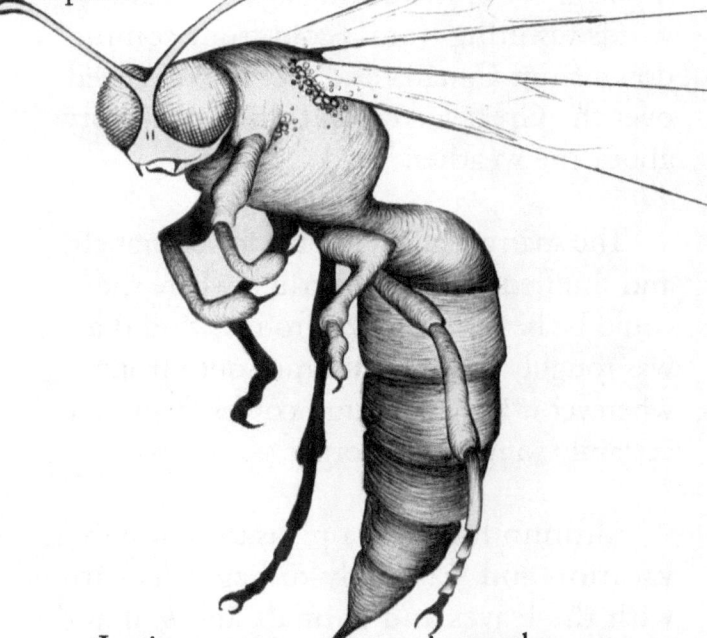

Juniper never gave it another thought, but she did have some soreness in her sepals for a few days.

The Bird and The Tree

Once upon a time, a tree was visited by a bird. Call it a sparrow. She was weary from a long flight, most of it working against headwinds resulting from a cold front coming down from Canada and picking up speed over the Great Lakes. But this isn't a story about the weather.

The sparrow alighted on a lower branch and shuffled towards the trunk where she could be better protected from a wind that was roughly pushing autumn south from wherever it is that autumn comes from, but certainly somewhere north.

Autumn had had a pleasant enough vacation and was ready to begin its turn with the leaves and animals and soil and sky for the next three-odd months. It was a big job.

Yes, all the seasons have comparably difficult jobs. They are also quite neurotic. Autumn is melancholic. She is the drunken poet of the seasons. Winter is the teetotaler, very serious, very spare. Spring is the manic one, the painter, hyperkinetic, indiscriminate with her absurd colors and insane lines. And summer is the loner, believe it or not. She brings heat like a Yankee pitcher, but stays to herself, wishing relief from herself: she knows she's too intense. It isn't healthy. But this story isn't about the seasons.

The sparrow shook herself. The tree could feel the cool air that the sparrow had brought with her. He sighed softly.

The nights would soon grow long and quiet and he could rest.

-Where are you coming from? he asked.

-Maine

-No kidding. Where's that?

-Up that way. The bird pointed north.

-Is that far?

-A couple hundred miles as the crow flies. That's a joke.

-What's a hundred? What's a mile? What's a crow? What's a joke? The sparrow shrugged. She thought, all these big branches and leaves, and a trunk that took centuries to build, and this tree is dumber than a box of lawyers.

The sparrow asked the tree what he did. She asked the tree what he knew. She asked him how he learned anything. Good questions.

-I have roots, he said. They go deep. They hear things in the earth.

This interested the sparrow.

-Like what?

-The motions of all the things moving around on this earth. And in. The steps of the deer, the gliding of the snake, the shifting of roots, the digging of moles.

-What does that teach you?

-I don't know because I don't know what I would know or wouldn't know without hearing those sounds.

-That's a point. What else?

-The voices of the unhappy ones.

-Who are they?

-They are the bodies that die and are unhappy about it, because they think they are leaving. They see only straight lines.

- How silly, said the bird.

- I hear them complain. When I listen to them, they seem to have done a lot of complaining when they were alive, too. The happy ones seem to die happy; the unhappy ones take their unhappiness with them into the earth.

-Do these unhappy ones ever become happy?

-No. Never.

-Say, that wind is really kicking up.

-Stay close. If you look up a bit, I have a little dent in my trunk. You can squeeze yourself in.

-I see it. The sparrow hopped up a few branches and slid into the niche in the trunk.

Suddenly, a branch snapped.

-Ouch.

-Are you okay?

-It happens all the time. Soon it will come back to me.

-What do you mean?

-Whatever I lose comes back. Leaves, twigs, branches: they fall to the earth, the earth takes them in, then my roots take them in, then up they go, back to being leaves, twigs and branches. Does it work that way for you?

-I don't think so. If I broke a wing, it would not come back to me. I would go away.

-Into the earth.

-Yes, into the earth.

-Then you might come back as part of me.

-If birds come back as trees, where do birds come from?

-I thought birds came from trees. Where else would they come from?

-That makes sense.

The wind blew strong the rest of the day and the following night. By morning, the air was calm. It was not without a certain sadness that the bird said goodbye to the tree.

-Perhaps we will meet again someday, she said.

-We will meet again someday. Perhaps the next time we meet, you shall be a tree and I shall be a bird.

The bird smiled - as well as a bird can smile - and thought the tree was pretty silly, after all. But she liked him nonetheless.

The Pumpkin Man,
The Stupid Man
and The Lantern Man

The Pumpkin Man, the Stupid Man, and the Lantern Man were sitting by the Pond of The Red Pixies, tossing the occasional pebble or twig into the water to see the ripples, only once in a while getting a harsh word from a twig or pebble that did not feel like getting tossed into the pond, when a raven landed before them.

Before the raven could begin to speak, an enchanted and wonderfully enlightened frog - Horace, in fact - returned one of the twigs to the land. The twig made a real ruckus about the rudeness of the men who thought it was all right to displace him with no consideration whatsoever.

The raven waited, shifting from one leg to the other, flapping as it grew impatient with the twig's diatribe. The Pumpkin Man apologized several times during the twig's bdelygmia; the Stupid Man threw his shoe at the twig; the Lantern Man puffed smoke from his head. When the twig was finished with his tirade, he hopped away into the woods, allowing them to turn their attention to the raven.

"I have a message from the queen," said the bird. "From the queen, I say. She wishes your presence on an urgent matter."

"Urgent, you say? From the queen, you say? Then we're off." But it was only a matter of a few steps before the Pumpkin Man realized that the magic forest was loaded - in fact, it was practically infested – with queens of the distressed variety.

"Raven, exactly which queen are we to see? The Queen of The Kind Heart, The Queen of The Lake of Blue Candles?

The Queen of The Hidden Tower? The Queen of The Lord King of Sumpferbourben? The Tiny-footed Queen of RubRub? The Bashful Queen? The Loud Queen? The…"

"The Queen of The Impressive Throne," said the raven with great pride and gravity, for there was no greater sovereign than she. (I ask you, is there ever?)

So the three bee-lined it to the Queen of The Impressive Throne. After the requisite bowing and scraping, the kissing of rings and asses, the walking backwards and bending forwards, she told them she had a gift of great value to bestow upon them: the glorious opportunity to please her. They would be the envy of the dead… er….the court.

Their task was to fight the dreaded Knight of The Unfailing And Fantastically Well-honed Double-edged Axe and liberate the queen's puppy, Randolfo, his captive. Her greatest soldiers had failed to do so, all seven thousand of them. So now it was the Pumpkin Man's chance to shine.

"Your highness, we are honored." And out they went.

The Lantern Man asked the plan.

The Pumpkin Man said, "Here is the plan: I can get us to the knight's castle in three days. I believe the Stupid Man can do better. He shall be our guide."

This was a master stroke: the Stupid Man's route managed to improve the duration of their trek by adding ninety-six years to it. Their timing was perfect: the dog was long dead; the knight was long dead; the queen was long dead; her court was long dead.

Their quest was by all accounts - or the three accounts that really mattered - a rousing success.

Thus ended, the Pumpkin Man, the Stupid Man and the Lantern Man found themselves back at the Pond of Red Pixies, tossing irritable twigs and vexed pebbles into the water to see the ripples.

The Mirror and
The Other Mirror

Once upon at time a mirror named Arora and another mirror named Neven co-existed on the same temporal, spatial and geometric planes sharing a superfluity of parallels. God, with his usual sense of humor and tape-measure-like precision, hung them on opposite walls in such a way that they faced each other perfectly.

They say opposites attract, but whoever they are, they certainly are not mirrors; for our reflective brethren, it was invariably like to like. Despite any superficial similarities between Arora and Neven - that is to say, the qualities observed by those insensitive to the keen particularities that make every mirror as unique as a crystalline snowflake - deep down, they were vide metaphora supra, as they say.

With mutual disinterest, they engendered an infinite number of mirrors through their cold intereaction. Like a bad date.

One day - neither of them knew after how many (a day to a mirror is a mere flicker) – something came between them: the image of a woman. She faced Arora; the back of her head was given to Neven. Their alignment yielded the usual infinity.

The woman looked very carefully into Arora, then began to cry. Arora and Neven proffered nothing except the multiplication of human sadness and frailty. Mirrors tend to be very insensitive.

Another head entered and proliferated. A man. The two heads became profiles. Suddenly, the silent world of the mirrors was shattered by the swing of a fist that struck Neven squarely in the locus. Neven's perfection was mathematized into fractal

chaos; his view was fractured and frag-
mented; mutual infinities were re-placed
with a private distorted geometry; his face
became the razor web of a mechanical spi-
der. Arora's reflection became irrelevant.

Being a mirror, she remained completely composed, despite what hung before her,
despite what was reflected inside her.

The man disappeared. The young
woman disappeared. Arora, as stated
above, was unfazed; Neven, however,
found himself far more interesting now.
He liked what he saw and he liked the
way he saw it. He decided that perhaps
we are too quick to abhor fractal chaos
when it is really no more than the mar-
riage of mathematics and a hammer. In
other words, Life.

Beware the judgment that causes us to
abhor fractal chaos.

The Troll's Promise

In a damp murky part of the magical forest, its floor dappled with exhausted sunlight, there stood a bridge. The function of this sorry structure was to carry one over a brook of icy water, that,

too, had traveled far, retaining its coldness over every rut, run, and turn. The bridge had been poorly made a long time before we come to it now, and time was not kind to it, as usual.

Beneath this bridge, always having one of his two enormous feet in the water, al-

ways bumping his lumpy head against the low- arched roof above him, lived a troll. His name was John Addlington Thomas, but he was generally referred to as The Hideous, Fanged Troll Who Lives Under The Bridge. Or John.

John had been living in that part of the magical forest long before the bridge was built by a charm of elves who had planned to make it their home, but became discouraged – even melancholy – by the unrelenting dreariness of the locale, so decided to move to a sunnier clime. Of course, the bridge stayed behind. If it could speak, it would have said that it was none too thrilled, especially after the Troll decided to make it his home. The bridge would tell you that the Troll was a slob. The brook would agree, being the recipient of his copious deposits, after which he would wipe his ass on one part or another of the bridge. He made no one happy.

The reason the Troll, um, *deposited* so generously was his diet, which consisted of anything he felt like eating because he despised its existence. He hated, for example, anything more attractive than he, which was pretty much everything. At the top of his hate list: puppies, kittens, princes and princesses, lost children, ponies, and talking frogs. But in a pinch anything with a pulse would do: skunks, hedgehogs, blister weavels, clog-rats, pustulous snakes, lepers, moles, night skinners, mud lizards, the usual soggy, enchanted forest fare.

That's the expository stuff. Now comes now.

One day the troll was sitting on a low rise from which he could look at his home, his bridge, when he saw a fox walking on his hind legs with admirable posture; that is to say, whose carriage was more trollpine than vulpine. He was also wearing pants, so he wouldn't feel so exposed walking upright like that. The pants had pockets, which is important for what happens later.

The Troll jumped up and ran to the bridge to stop the fox before he could cross. "No one crosses my bridge without paying a toll," he said.

"Why should I pay a toll to you when I could just walk across the stream? So what if my paws get a bit wet. Fur dries, you know."

"The short answer is, I would eat you before the water hit your skinny little ankles."

"That's a good argument for paying the toll, my friend. What's the damage?"

"For you….well, what do you have?"

"The odd coin, a talisman or two, a bit of tree bark, a twitch of purple grass, a thorn given to me by a friend, a bit of dried molasses shaped into a ball. That's about it.'

The Troll scratched and thought. "Well, then…the price for crossing this bridge is that bit of tree bark. It's a fine-looking specimen."

"It was a gift for a job well done. I cherish it for its sentimental value."

"That's the price," insisted the troll.

"And nothing else will do?"

"I don't make the rules."

They both shook their heads at this. "Alas," mused the fox philosophically, "who does make the rules?"

The troll sighed and shrugged, then began honing his black teeth with a whetstone he had 'borrowed' from a witch's house. The fox was able to read this subtle sign.

"Okay," said the fox, "the bit of tree bark. But if you would, if you could, please make a promise to me so I don't feel so terrible about losing this gift."

"I'm not very good with promises."

"And yet here you are being honest as the rain. You may be a better fellow than you think. So: take this bit of tree bark as your toll. Put it away. Do not sell it. Do not trade it. Perhaps some day I shall return this way and you will allow me to buy it back at a price you deem fair."

The troll gave this serious thought. At last he said, "Done. Have a nice day." And with a sweep of his arm, he let the fox pass over the bridge.

If there were such a thing as a clock or a calendar in the enchanted forest, it could be said with confidence that three hundred years and seven hours had passed when the fox returned to the bridge, this time, of course, from the other side. If there were such a thing as a footnote in this enchanted forest it would say there is no significance to this period of time, though some meaning seems to be suggested.

They knew each other right away, as if no time had passed at all. It was as if the fox just suddenly appeared on the other side of the bridge. As if, really, someone had just turned from looking at the reflection of a picture of a troll, a fox and a bridge in a mirror to looking directly at the picture. A mere turn of the head. Amazing.

"Welcome back, fox."

"Hello again, troll. Do you have my bit

of bark? I have, I believe, an item of great value to barter with."

"Okay."

"I have a magic stone. The story of this stone would astound you should you care to know it."

"Listen, everything around here is magic. Magic stones, magic trees, magic fountains, magic cows, beans, flowers, butterflies. Why don't you just tell me what this magic stone does?"

"It grants you a wish."

"No kidding? A wish! Well, I'll be damned." (Trolls can be quite sarcastic.) "I'll take the ball of dried molasses."

"Okay," said the fox, "but I'm going to tell you right now that if you don't take the stone, I'm going to use it and wish for my bit of tree bark back."

"Why didn't you just do that in the first place?"

"I like to be fair."

The Troll recalled: "Once there was a king named Midas...or was it a mouse? Well, if there wasn't, there will be. If you were to ask him the value of gold, he would answer with tears. Keep your stone. Take it far from here. You should be smart enough to know that nothing yields discontent faster than a wish fulfilled." The troll turned, took a step back and said, "Begone!" which is magic-forest talk for hit the bricks.

When the fox was far from the bridge, he took out the stone and threw it far, far into the deep, wet forest. If you're interested, it still sits exactly where it landed.

The troll walked to his favorite place on the knoll, spotted a cute little squirrel working on an acorn, took the gentle creature into his hand and popped it into his mouth. The fur tickled for a moment or two, until he swallowed it, acorn and all.

The Ant and
Some Kind of Bird

Once there lived an ant named Gaul, an admirably hard-working fellow who came from a long line of hard-working ants. He lived in the shade of a plant named Dryopteris filix-mas. Both Gaul and Dryopteris liked moist but well-drained soil, long walks on the beach, and a nice Cabernet, not too fruity. Gaul was not as much of a social butter-fly as most ants are; he preferred to work alone rather than sandwiched between two others of his kind, marching back and forth from barracks to decomposing firefly until the latter was completely translated into the former. Oh, he'd do the work all right, but he marched alone.

One day Gaul had followed some chemical marker to a dead field mouse. There were plenty of other of ants there already, striping the carcass like a carnivorous car wash. Gaul did something that ants never do: he stopped.

What did stopping actually entail? The jittery, agitated, jerky mimesis of a crack-and-caffeine-induced palsy was replaced by a complete and perfect stillness. He looked dead and when an ant isn't moving, he may as well be. A motionless ant is food for the rest of the ant population. Ants are too efficient to ignore nutriment that is sitting right in front of them.

One could argue that his separation from his species caused him to forget the mores that guide them. These mores include the laws of their nature, suitable salutations to acquaintances, the proper seating order at formal dinners, how to write a condolence letter, how to address an invitation to your boss, and so on, that are essential for their survival. Gaul had been out of touch too long, perhaps, and was now a lost soul. This may sound obvious but an ant's identity depends upon his acting like an ant. In fact, it depends on his acting like every ant.

A bird flew down from a nearby hedge-row, thinking the obvious and preparing to eat the ant. Her shadow stirred the ant who glared at the bird with naive defiance.

But the bird was amused. She landed beside the ant and asked him why he was playing possum.

"I'm not playing possum. I'm just...." The ant searched for the right words, but there are none in ant language that convey the meaning of motionlessness.

"What?"

"I was heading over to get some field mouse and I could smell that there was already a good-sized crowd there. Suddenly, I just wasn't hungry enough."

"I thought ants were always hungry. All that moving, moving, moving."

"You guys, too."

"We sleep. We rest. I've never seen an immobile ant. So I figured you were dead."

"I envy you, flying."

"You know, I never grow tired of it. Sometimes I fly just…to fly. I float around up there and when I land I'm almost disappointed."

"Ants don't do anything like that. We aren't what you would call free spirits. Think you could take me up?"

"I guess I could, but how would you hold on?"

"If I can walk upside down on a slippery phone wire swinging in the wind during a thunderstorm, I should be able to hold on. Maybe under your neck somewhere."

"Okay. Climb on."

And he did.

He never ever wanted to come back to earth.

In the profound peace of the sky he began to anticipate the misery of the land below. This proleptic misery would prove accurate.

When they landed, he thanked the bird and waved as well as he could as he took off again.

Gaul crawled home and resigned himself to his terrestrial limitations: north, east, south, west. Sure, down a little and up a little, too, but the heights he would never again reach! How small was he and how big the world!

Gaul was never the same. He stayed home, stopped eating, and became a dry, brittle, living corpse of an ant, then a dead one.

His last dream was that he was far up in the air looking below on what had once been - almost - enough.

The Old Man
and The Star

Once upon a time in a little town that could be reached only by a single path that wound round and round an enormous mountain, there lived a very old man. Few people visited this old man – or anyone else in this town – because it was invisible to those below, blocked as it was by the clouds that floated beneath it. You would have to be very old to remember the town was even there. But the people who lived there didn't mind: they lived their lives in simple content-ment, working and talking and remem-bering lives that were very much their own. In the cool evenings, they would sit on their porches, swathed in heavy blankets, the circle of razor-radiant stars wrapped around them, and talk.

Looking up, one imagined the stars, too, were talking to each other. They sparkled and blazed and shone in their brilliant secret syntax, in their singing celestial voices, in the fire-and-ice vocabulary of the empyrean, the music of the spheres, the quintessential harmony. They drank tea, rocked gently in chairs or swings, in their own magic blanket.

The very old man was not the oldest in this little town. He was perhaps third or fourth. A few were so old they could not precisely remember their ages; after all, how important is such knowledge? And though they could not remember their years, they could remember the time when the stars were configured differently, when the world spun more slowly, when the sun rose on the other side and when very different animals hid under their porches, pawed at the moon or flew overhead.

He had a still. He drew sap from certain trees and drew out roots from deep in the black earth mixed and titrated into precious drink.

One night - on one of his myriad birthdays - a star came down from above - actually, from across - to visit him. This star ran a streaming horizontal from its position in the celestial screen to the old man's porch where he was sitting, a bottle of green winter stroop in his hand.

The old man had followed the perfect line of the star as it came towards him, closer and closer yet never growing larger. Stars are funny that way.

When it finally arrived, the old man patted the step he was sitting on and invited the star to join him.

"So," said the old man.

"So," said the star, resting on the step, reclining in imitation of his host. Both looked up at the sky.

"Nice," said the old man.

"Very," said the star.

"Swig?" asked the old man.

"Thank you. Because it's your birthday."

"Do you have a birthday?"

"I do. Thank you for asking."

"Could you tell me?"

"It is the same as yours. It is today."

"And your age...."

"The same as well."

"Then let us toast our birthday together. And to our health."

They took turns at the bottle. It may have been the effect of the liquor or their general happiness, but the star began to shine even brighter. The old man began to shine brighter as well. Both smiled and beamed and felt the warmth.

There was no need to fill each moment with words; the two were comfortable in silence as well as in sound. When the bottle was empty they knew this time was ended.

"There is a hole in the sky. That is the place I left and for which I am responsible. Darkness cannot be left unattended for too long or it will spread. So."

"Well, old friend, I am glad you came. And I hope we will meet again some time."

"We will. And we will share another bottle then."

The star began to rise, but it was the old man who took off. The beaming visitor watched as the old fellow retraced the faintly luminous path that the star had made to the old man's porch. And the star knew when the old man had reached his destination, for the hole in the sky disappeared and a blazing light shone again. No, blazing is too sharp; lambent is closer: for this new-old star glowed with a warmth that could be felt from very far away.

The star smiled and shrugged. He picked up the empty bottle and staggered a bit, wobbled a bit, up the steps to the door. He wondered how long it would be before he would get the feel of gravity.

Before retiring for the night, he blew out the candle on the nightstand, the flame dancing briefly before going dark.

The Secret of The Black Tree

Once there was a Black Tree, a dark, evil tree that was as cruel as it was ageless. Some say it grew straight from the stomach of the devil. Sometimes it was less a tree than a giant chimneystack; its leaves and branches were thick black smoke; its trunk was hard and cold as the devil's heart. Anything that drew too close to this terrible tree would be caught in its gloom and would die. Man or wolf, squirrel or snake: all would be trapped in its inexorable pitch.

For miles around this tree, the earth was black and lifeless. The dirt was without life; not a worm or grub to be found; not a single blade of grass; not a footprint. Occasionally, a stray wind would brush

this dead land, but once it passed, there was nothing but choking stillness. But not quiet, for the great tree would shift itself and the ground would quake and the sickening, arthritic motion of the tree would cause it to groan in agony. It was as if the tree could not decide the greater pain: that of movement or of stillness.

And the groans of that tree would travel to towns and villages many miles away; children would shudder in their sleep, adults would shift uneasily, and dogs would whimper and hide when those sounds found them.

Boys and girls, if only this were a tale where a brave lumberjack would cut down that hideous tree or some princess would bring light to the black land or some good child would lay a trail of love that would grow into a road of white roses...

Do you think that every tale should have in it a road of white roses? Or a brave lumberjack? Or a beautiful princess? Alas, this is not such a tale.

But there are in this little story a not-so-brave shepherd and a not-so-pretty spinning-maid who found themselves walking on a road that was certainly the wrong road for the attainment of their destination. In fact the sign said, "Wrong Road," but since neither could read, it didn't much matter.

And though he was dumber than a sack of sand and she was dopier than a bucket of turnips, together they were able to not walk into trees or ditches. For better or worse - and philosophers have discoursed for centuries about this - their colossal ignorance took them will-nilly to the edge of the land of the Black Tree.

The threshold wasn't hard to notice, for right in the middle of the day, everything went dark. In the span of one step, day turned into starless, moonless night; one step backward, they discovered, turned night into full day again. They exulted at this find, stepping into and out of night over and over, jumping and hopping into day again and again. Back and forth, night and day, until it was night on both sides. Then they went to sleep.

When they awoke, they again had the two halves of the diurnal cycle to choose from. They again did their imbecilic to-and-fro for hours, then - almost miraculously - set forth again in the direction of the deadly tree. Soon the black dust turned into black mud and then into black muck.

Here it should be noted that the shepherd was a lanky, underfed lad, your typical bag of bones, as they say; and the spinning-maid was a mere wisp of a girl, so thin as to be almost weightless. And both were blessed with enviably empty heads. These qualities allowed him to travel farther than most into the Black Tree's circle since he was unburdened with the kind of gravity that would sink another man, and she practically floated over the sea of mud beneath her.

They barely felt the muck on their soles. The bleakness that surrounded them; the sad thoughts that one would think unavoidable; the oppressiveness of the elements, of the air, itself: none of this could permeate their aura of blissful noodlehood.

The tree watched them. If it could have spewed a thicker, more noxious blackness from its trunk, it would have; if it could have oozed blacker lava from its roots, it would have; if it could have blasted greater waves of evil, of misery, of desolation, of pain from its ramage, it would have. Evil, black-hearted trees have big egos: their thirst is unquenchable. And these two idiots were levitating right past it.

Soon, the shepherd lad and the spinning girl had traveled through the black land. Soon, too, the Black Tree was able to shrug off the inconsiderate behavior of the oblivious pair. You can't win 'em all.

The lad and the girl grew up, grew old, and died.

The tree, of course, will always be.

The Little Family and The Visitor

Once upon a time there was a quiet and happy family that lived deep in the forest. They had few possessions yet never felt need. Their house was a small, sturdy cabin; there was a single table with five chairs, for there were five of them; there were five straw beds; there were several spoons and knives and bowls and such; and little else worthy of notice.

One summer's day, as the four children were gathering wood for the fire and the mother was kneading dough to make bread, there was a sudden gust of cold wind that made them all shiver as much from surprise as from the chill. Something cold tickled the nose of the littlest one; it was a snowflake. And many more followed. The children saw their mother standing on the steps wrapped in her shawl, looking up to see where snow could be coming from. The sun shone, there were no clouds, the leaves moved in gentle waves in the breeze:

all the signs of the vernal season were present, ignorant of the cold and snow coming not from above but from the east.

And then came the thunder. Mother and children huddled now inside their home for the thunder was certainly coming in their direction, louder and louder until the children covered their ears. Then it stopped. The quiet was an uneasy one.

It lasted for but a moment, for there was a knock on the door that was chilling for its suddenness. The children were more curious than scared; the mother shared these feelings, except for the curiosity. She wiped her apron, took a breath and opened the door.

There stood Winter. Behind was a clear swath of snow and ice that led directly to the bottoms of his boots.

Now you are probably as curious as the

children were to know what Mr. Winter or
Lord Winter or King Winter - whatever the
appropriate title - looked like. He certainly
did not look like a snowman or anything
ridiculous like that. He certainly was not
dressed from head to toe in a white cos-
tume. Nor did he have a long hoary beard.
He was tall and a bit stooped, tired looking,
old to the children but less so to the mother.
His hair was grey, his eyes light, light blue,
his chin unshaven. No hat. His face looked
as if it used to smile often, but was now a
bit more sober if not somber. The family
found it to be a likable face.

"May I...?" His motions were small, his
voice was strong but not loud.

"Yes, yes," said the mother, "do please
come in."

Winter stepped across the threshold and
his season came with him. The children
ran to wrap themselves in blankets and
scarves and ran back to watch the fellow sit
at their table.

"If you keep the door open, it will let out some of the cold. I apologize for the weather."

"Nonsense, sir. May we offer you something? We have stew and I am baking bread."

"A bowl of something warm would be nice."

At the first sip from the spoon, mist appeared to rise from the floorboards. With the second, the ice from the eaves began to melt. With each taste, the cabin grew warmer. The children discarded their blankets and stood to watching. The mother apologized.

"I have children, too," said the visitor. They are good for the heart."

"What brings you here, if you can say?" asked the mother.

One of the children spoke: "Sir, are you Winter?" Another asked, "Or, sir, are you Death?"

The mother gave a scolding look. The child said, "Sir, I mean no insult, but you are kind and you are cold. Our father once told us that Death is such. If you are, do you know him, my father?"

"No, child, I am Winter. Death is a cousin. Though we are much alike, as you say, yet you receive us differently. You see me and do not fear me for you know my sister, Spring, will bring the world around. Yet you do not trust Death's sister to do the same. Why do you believe in Spring's promise, but not in Life's? If you saw them standing together you would think they were twins, though Spring has hair green as the leaves, and Life has hair the color of the sun at dawn."

The children marveled. The oldest gave these words great thought.

"Why have you come? And in the middle of summer?" asked the mother.

"I have come for your stew."

"You tease me, sir."

"Even Winter needs warmth occasionally, so I came to you."

The family did not know what to say. They felt sorry for the fellow who now glowed, showing no vestige of his season.

"You are always welcome here, " said the mother.

"I don't know how to thank you, for I know you would ask for nothing. But I leave you the smallest of gifts for my gratitude. He took out a little white kerchief, unfolded it and laid it on the table. He called the children over. "Look." He touched the kerchief and it was no longer a bit of square cloth, but a tiny field of fresh snow, bright and glistening.

He took a pinch of snow and flicked it through the window. "Now look."

When the children ran to the window they saw a small field of newly-fallen snow.

"I leave this with you, should you crave a bit of cold sometime. And now I shall thank you again and take my leave." He folded the cloth and gave it to the mother who placed it in her apron pocket.

The effect of the warm meal began to fade, and as the children watched Winter walk from the house, each step brought more snow around him. When he had disappeared, the snow did too, and Summer was all around them.

That winter it was Summer's turn to visit, and her gift was a patch of cloth of the greenest hue.

The Gnome and
The Hobgoblin

Once upon a time there was a gnome whose job it was to guard the vast treasure of King Ogre, who lived inside an enormous mountain of rock on which only the hideous clench-thorn grew and only the horrendous six-legged spit-spat lived. Then there was the cold, ceaseless rain.

There was one entrance to the King's dwelling within the cave: a long, deep tunnel that was horrifyingly dark and filled with ugly, evil, vile, despicable, gruesome, grotesque, monstrous, sickening, murderous creatures of every kind. A short list should suffice:

The mordragon, a two-headed serpent that would grab its victim by the throat with one set of jaws and allow the other head to slide down the victim's throat to eat him inside-out, like a carnivorous laryngoscope.

The scabwallok, who would rip the flesh off its enemy and suck out its brains through its eye sockets, like marrow from a chicken bone.

The trolp, who would dig the long spidery fingers of his five hands into his prey and then slowly pull him apart, like taffy.

The fire weasel who would jump onto the face of its target, pierce the eyes with its long claws, and then spit fire into the skull, cooking the brains and then eating them while the body of the poor sufferer writhed in agony.

At the entrance of this tunnel stood the gnome, giving the appearance of a clay homunculus crushed, twisted and squeezed into his present form. He was strong and tough as a giant's anvil. He carried a serrated sword with edges filled with bits of bone and flesh; a ferocious dagger; and a battered, bloodstained pike. He enjoyed ripping with his teeth, the ears and noses from those who came too close. Not enjoyed so much as relished.

He was undefeated in nearly eleven thousand challenges.

Then came the hobgoblin, a pointy-eared, pointy-toothed, pointy-tongued, pointy-winged, pointy-tailed demon to steal King Ogre's treasure. He, too, was undefeated. He, too, loved his work.

The gnome saw him coming up the steep hill, practically skipping over the skulls and bones littering the path. Was he singing?

The hobgoblin stopped just short of the length of the bloody pike.

The gnome wasn't much of a conversationalist because of a nasty speech impediment; the goblin, however, would talk your ear off if he could. Literally.

"Hello, gnome. I'm here for Ogre's gold."

The gnome, beginning to drool, replied with a playful lunge of the pike. The goblin stepped back, put on his scary face, flew into the air, extended his claws, and dove at the gnome. The gnome met him with his dagger in one hand and his sword in the other.

Clouds of dust and rock billowed into the air, mixed with bits of flesh, scales, teeth, hair, spit, blood and thick sweat. Until the evening of the second day.

As the gnome was retracting a digit from the hobgoblin's eye socket, he suggested a break. The loss of half his upper lip actually improved his enunciation.

"I'm in." said the goblin.

They rested.

"Nice view," noted the goblin.

"You start taking it for granted somewhere," replied the gnome. "Been doing this long, have you?"

"I've been here longer than those trees there." He pointed to a wall of redwoods whose enormous trunks rose to the clouds. The goblin leaned over the edge of the ridge to see where they began, then followed them up, up, up. The boughs were a rich, glowing green.

The bleak mountain could never overshadow them.

"And you?"

"It's in my blood, I guess." The goblin kicked a skull into one of the mounds of bones around them. "I'm not much for anything else."

"You fare well enough."

"It's not what it used to be. Or I'm not what I used to be. Sometimes in the middle of a fight I find myself thinking of other things. Distant things."

"Maybe it's time to call it quits."

"Maybe after this one." They both smiled.

Gnomes and hobgoblins have this in common: they never quit. After they had rested a bit longer, they rose as if in response to some signal and resumed their battle. After another day of fighting, they rested again.

"This is one for the books,' said the gnome.

"You're not kidding. You don't happen to have any food around? I mean, like an apple or bread, not like a knight or anything like that."

"Bread. Yes. The gnome walked to the tunnel entrance, disappeared and reappeared with a loaf of bread."

At the end of the third day, they rested again. And after the fourth, the same. The gnome had lost his left hand and both ears. The goblin, an eye, three fingers, and half of a foot. The fifth day was not pretty.

"I will have the Ogre's treasure," declared the goblin. His voice was weak.

"I understand," said the gnome. There was something between compassion and resignation in his voice.

Both were nearly blind. They limped sadly towards each other, the goblin with a rock in his hand, the gnome with his dagger. The sword had been broken two days earlier. They didn't so much lunge as fall into each other, slashing and smashing as best they could. The dagger had done much

to the goblin, but goblins tolerate pain.
After crushing the rock against the gnome's
head several times, the dagger found its
way up into the goblin's neck. This time,
the gnome did not pull the dagger out, but
drove it deeper and deeper, twisting and
driving and drilling until his hand was lost
under the flesh of the combatant.

The gnome felt the full weight of the
goblin on him. It was done. He dragged
the body to the side of the tunnel and
sat beside it.

"No treasure for you, I'm afraid.
Though you deserved more than a loaf
of bread for your efforts. But that's all
you get, sometimes. I shall not eat you. I
will bury you, instead, under those trees.
Five days." For some reason, the gnome
laughed. "Five days, you goblin."

Gnomes have incredible recuperative
powers. A year later, his hand, his eye, and his
ears had grown back. He had healed entirely,
though he was still unmistakably a gnome.

Not long after, a knight in golden armor came for King Ogre's treasure anxious to do battle. But there would be none, for the gnome was doing some whittling beneath the redwoods in a patch of light.

The gnome knew the well-groomed challenger was up there, nor was the irony lost to him that this shining knight was a lesser adversary than the hobgoblin; that the gnome was now the guardian of the Copse of Great Trees, a more valuable treasure; that the knight who was lucky not to have to face the gnome would in fact be foolish enough to be disappointed; that this disappointment was justified nonetheless, for the knight would never be remembered.

When he finished his carving, the gnome tossed it onto the pile of similar little ornaments he had shaped from bits of wood that adorned the grave of the noble and worthy hobgoblin.

The Princess and The Prince

Once upon a time there was an unfulfilled prince and princess who sat around in the royal garden holding hands and feeling about as much passion as the marble statues that surrounded them. He had been sent to her country to marry her because their union would prevent a war. If there is a better reason for two people to marry, please let us know.

So they sat. And sat. And for a change of pace, they perambulated. Their togetherness was an altogether uninspiring affair, so much so that the birds dozed, the squirrels snored, the flowers hung over each other like exhausted pugilists, and the footmen and maidens pondered suicide.

Not that the princess and the prince weren't good looking. They were perfect in form. And if pressed for conversation, they could hold their own. Nor were they cursed with unusually large egos; they were neither more nor less vain than the royalty next door. They were simply a pair of lovely bookends; functional but - no, not but - functional because they were inert.

"Does it bother you that we are just furniture?" she asked him, as the day of their wedding approached.

"Sorry?"

"I said, does it bother you that we are just pieces of furniture, built and placed to serve our purpose, like two chairs in a salon?"

"I can't say that it bothers me, really. I suppose there are worse things."

"Worse than being furniture?"

"Unlike furniture, we are able to travel anywhere we like, with an entourage of fifty maids and valets and guards and secretaries and such. Let's see a divan say that!" he said triumphantly.

The princess called the prince a twerp (in her head, naturally, so as not to violate decorum).

The night before the day of her wedding, the princess decided to drink a lot of wine. After doing that, she decided to run into the garden and kiss every frog she could find. She then kissed one of the palace guards, a strong, tall, silent fellow who never saw it coming.

Despite her imploring, he was arrested, shackled and beheaded the next day, her wedding day.

Another jeroboam of wine was clearly in order.

As she walked toward the altar, she decided to kiss every guard who lined the walkway. Everyone was appalled. The humiliation! The expense! The beheadings! But she just kept tiptoeing to reach the lips of each man, each man tightening his lips in hopes of avoiding decapitation. The ambassadors seemed to have their pants on fire judging from the way they ran to mount their horses. The scandal was too delicious. The prince was not terribly concerned. Furniture, indeed!

War was declared and when all was done thousands died, thousands were wounded, thousands widowed, thousands orphaned, thousands of farms burned, thousands of ounces of gold and silver lost. The prince was sent to lead an army and was killed. The princess was now worthless on the open market; she became a spinster and eventually somebody's crazy aunt.

The desire for passion is common, but it is an expensive commodity and better left to those who have nothing to lose.

The Princess and
The Magic Closet

Once upon a time there was a beautiful princess who loved herself because she was beautiful. She thought so, her parents thought so, her subjects thought so, every prince who ever saw her thought so.

So we can reasonably assume she was the genuine article.

One day while she was gazing at herself in her mirror, she saw something ghastly. It was - dare we say it? - the first tiny hint of a microscopic suggestion of a near-invisible intimation of the most minute line on the outside corner of her left eye.

She called her attendants. She called the court physicians. She called her advisors. No one saw what she saw. Or so they said; when acknowledging a wrinkle is tantamount to requesting to be hanged, one does the wise thing and keeps one's mouth shut.

There was one wizened counselor to the king who offered her some advice.

"Princess, though I cannot say that I see what it is that distresses you, it is understandable that you fear what inevitably comes. There is one fellow I know who can stave off this thing. His name is Pitchbarron and he lives in the magical forest. I can take you to him, if you wish."

That is what one calls a no-brainer.

One day later, the counselor, the princess and Pitchbarron were sitting outside of his home in the forest. Pitchbarron explained that he did indeed have the solution to the princess' problem, but it would cost her a great deal. She thought he was talking about money and he was fine with that misunderstanding. She filled his pockets with gold coins.

Pitchbarron then took her into a room that held dozens of huge cabinets. Each was of a different type of wood and richly engraved with all kinds of strange signs and inscriptions. Each had a single door.

He led her to one that looked positively funereal and said, "This is The Closet of Eternal Youth. When you are in it, you will not age a single second. The more time you spend in it, the longer you will retain your perfect, flawless beauty. Except, of course, for that unfortunate little wrinkle by your eye. What a shame you didn't come to me sooner."

The princess was thrilled. She practically jumped into the cabinet and pulled the door closed.

The counselor asked her if she was all right. He was feeling a bit iffy about the whole thing; he could see (as she could not) that these closets had a disconcerting similarity to certain caskets he had seen on his voyages to distant lands.

She said she had never been happier, though it was a bit cramped. She asked if she could have a little stool to sit on. Pitchbarron found one, knocked on the door and then opened it to give it to her.

"Much better."

A few hours later, she stepped out.

"How do I look?"

Pitchbarron looked up from his soup. "Exactly as you did when you went in. But be careful, I can see that you are already beginning to age again.

She ran back into the closet. Pitchbarron went back to his soup.

And that was that. She never came out again. We must therefore assume she lived happily ever after.

The Blacksmith and
The Billy Goat

Once upon a time…no, even before that…..

In the magic forest there lived a blacksmith. Yes, just then.

He made everything from hairpins to horseshoes. His smithy contained dozens of anvils, hammers of every size and shape and weight, several and various tongs, hardies and swages, and two - count 'em! - two forges.

There wasn't much work, despite his being the only blacksmith in the forest, except of course for Vulcan, way down in the other direction.

(This is not a reference to some retired old god; no one said this Vulcan was the Roman deity. Interesting how names can throw people off.) His hammering - naturally - sounded like thunder; the sparks were like lightning; his face was covered with thick soot streaked with sweat; his eyes were obsidian encircled with fire. He would set his teeth - half-grimace, half-smirk - flattening a bar of iron with one stroke that would take two score from anyone else. He worked the hammer as if he were trying to prove something; he dared the metal to resist him.

But our blacksmith did not see metal as defiant; to him it was malleable and cooperative. (It really is how you see the world.)

The elements - fire and earth and air and water - would crash and converge in violent harmony, and they would join to all sorts of things. Sparks and steam and sweat and steel could merge into anything.

The bits, buckles, stirrups, tankards, plates, swords, shields, breastplates, razors, plow points, hitches, knobs, spoons and anything else needing iron or steel or tin were shaped into their essence, then tossed onto a huge pile.

And now we segue from the sublime to the goat that needed a new bell.

The clapper - the thing inside the bell that swings back and forth striking the shell to make the ringing sound - was lost. Which means it was no longer a bell, just a metal cup hanging upside down around the neck of a goat. The ignominy. For all parties, really.

To lend to the gravity of the matter - as if that's even necessary - it was a magic bell.

This is how the goat came to have a magic bell around his neck (the short version):

A beautiful young girl found that bell half-buried in a creek and discovered that it granted wishes when she gave it a quick buff with her sleeve. (How it got into that creek, we'll never know.) Being young and beautiful - and smarter than just about anyone else in the universe - she figured she had nothing to wish for: she was already young and beautiful. What was left?

She decided to be rid of it to keep it out of the hands of people far less wise than she. She took the approach of hiding it in plain sight by tying it to just any old goat that ambled by. That was this goat.

So much for any such plans working out in the forest. There's just too much enchanted stuff going on. It's sort of like the whole clash and convergence thing mentioned above: all those elements will come together - it is magical, really - and create new things. To make a short story shorter: the goat was an enchanted goat; the clapper fell off; the goat went straight to the blacksmith.

The goat spoke to the blacksmith: "Sir, if you have time, could you shape a new ringer for this bell?"

"Easy enough." The blacksmith had been hammering a helmet for a basilisk, but he set it aside and walked over to the goat to examine the former bell. He began to unfasten it, but the goat objected: "Must you remove it?"

"I suppose not," said the smith. He found a small piece of iron, cut and filed and hammered it, tested the size and shape inside the bell, did some more cutting and filing and hammering, and so on, until it was done.

The goat was grateful; the sound was pleasant. He offered payment to the blacksmith, who said it was not necessary. (Like a goat has pockets, anyway.)

As the goat returned to his pasture he wondered if the bell still had its power. (He knew the story.) Then he wondered how - or if - he should test it. Then he wondered if it really mattered. But how could it not with all that history? That's a lot of vacillation for a goat.

He decided that he would take an oath to make just one wish, because he knew that wishes were a) very tricky and b) incredibly habit-forming.

Just to test the magical waters, so to speak, he wished that the bell had never broken.

When nothing happened - or nothing seemed to happen - the goat smiled. (Sure, goats can smile. They have a terrific sense of humor, especially for the absurd.) Then he headed for his favorite field accompanied by the reassuring sound of the little bell.

The Princess &
The Whole
Stinking World

Once upon a time there was a princess who would mope around bemoaning the whole stinking world. Often, she would find a tree stump somewhere and sit on it, digging her shoes into the soil, kicking the odd stone or twig, slam her little fist into her knee, and huff and puff. It wasn't a bad routine.

Boy, did the world stink! It was a boring, putrid, rotten, stupid, dumb, dull - did we mention boring? - world. Sometimes she could just scream. Really.

And her parents, the king and queen, were without a doubt the worst parents in the whole stinking world. They were so strict and unreasonable and stupid that it was a wonder they could manage an entire kingdom. Yet their subjects were even dumber; they practically worshiped His and Her Majesties; these imbeciles thought their kingdom was being run just fine. Where do people like this come from? Eggs? The cows had more sense.

One day, after she yelled at her chambermaids, threw her breakfast plate at the kitchen girl, kicked her valet in the shin, and positively wilted the pride of the stable hands with a litany of profanity that made the nearby manure fragrant by comparison, she stomped off to the woods.

With her hands clenched in little white fists (making her knuckles a nasty red) she pounded through the forest. Bunnies and does and hummingbirds headed for the hills pronto. A brown bear made the mistake of getting in her way. A wolf - a veteran when it came to dealing with the fair sex - tried to approach her; she tore him a new one.

She found her favorite - or least despised - tree stump and sat, assuming her habit of pushing the dirt with her feet, digging deep ruts with the heels of her embroidered gold and silver slippers. Suddenly, she found her feet stuck. She tried to pull her feet back, but couldn't. She managed to stand and then tried to raise her feet, but couldn't do that either.

"Okay," she said, "What is going on here?" She didn't so much say it as growl it. "I'm not kidding. Whoever's doing this better stop."

(The world did not intend to punish her by holding her. It thought it could get the princess to pull herself together. What a funny little world to think this.)

Her lip curled up (never a good sign) and she stopped trying to pull her feet out and instead began pushing and digging deeper into the earth, with a vengeance.

The world - that selfsame stinking world - would have scratched its head in wonder at such behavior, except that the princess was scratching it for him. What was this creature doing? Surely she wasn't creating furrows for planting; nor was she digging for something to build with; nor was she seeking something with which she could carve or mold to create something new; nor was she digging a home for herself, like the mole or the mouse. The world wasn't comfortable with this useless behavior. Actions were supposed to have purpose.

Meanwhile, the princess kept pushing and twisting, adding a new dimension by simultaneously yanking at her hair, pulling it up, down and sideways. If electricity existed in that neck of the woods, one would have thought she brushed her hair with it.

By nightfall, she had dug herself in over her skinny calves. Her dress of silk and pearls was a frightful, muddy mess.

Well, boys and girls, surely we can see where this is going. By sunrise, she would no longer be an angry, silly princess. Rather, she would be a weak, wispy, drab little tree. And someday, a handsome prince on a handsome steed seeking a beautiful princess to marry and to make wonderfully happy for ever and ever, would come by. His perfectly appointed horse would pause by this very tree - heart be still! - and liberally relieve itself before moving on.

Sometimes we take part in the making of our destinies.

The Witch and
The Clock

Once upon a time there was a witch who lived in a small cottage that belied her powers. If you're a witch who does not suffer from low self-esteem, why would you need anything ostentatious? On the other hand, could it hurt to add an extra room or two?

In her home were the usual witchly appurtenances and paraphernalia: a rocking chair; shelves of vials, phials, jars and boxes; a chimney with a black cauldron; a rack of long spoons for stirring and tasting; a broomstick; half-dozen wands; a conical hat; a black cat; an owl; mice; small table; two stepstools for little visitors; several mirrors; and an enormous clock.

The witch was smart enough to keep the mirrors as far from the clock as possible, for she knew that of all the terrible combinations, that of the clock and the mirror was by far the worst; frightening to

behold, their victims were numberless and
their fates sad beyond measure. If there is
a better example of incompatibility than
Vanity and Time, please write. Time is the
unrelenting sculptor who won't stop until
the marble block is dust.

But enough negativity: if you turn your
attention to the window, just outside you
will see twitching bunnies, fluffy clouds,
beneficent fairies and weightless butterflies
dancing on summer breezes.

The witch was not a negative person.
She had been around too long. Live long
enough and every emotion and attitude
becomes tempered to an admirable Aristo-
telian mean. Even fear.

(The only uncompromising emotion,
no matter how much you've lived, is love;
you can never get the reins on it: that's why
god gives old people cataracts.)

The clock.

The clock did not work. Not because it existed in a timeless place. And not because of the absurdity of being the only clock in the land. (Like language, it takes at least two to give any justification to their mediums.) It did not work because the witch had stilled the pendulum - some say - with an icy stare, which isn't true at all. But you know rumors.

So it stood in silence, a sentinel, stiff-backed, noble and still, seven feet tall, which made it three feet taller than the witch.

The clock was an existential masterpiece. When the witch sat in her rocking chair and looked at it, she pondered things that would never occur to her if she were looking at a cow or an elf.

She wondered if it was the stillness of the clock that made it so profound to her.

And of course, mirrors provoked thoughts; but the conjunction of a clock and a mirror...well, it's better just to make sure it doesn't happen. Don't even think about it.

One warm day, the smell of gingerbread wafted into the witch's house, the result of the sun warming the sugary tiles of the neighbor's house just down the ill-worn path. The witch was idly stirring a potion to a slow boil, her mind wandering here and there, and for whatever reason - the summer breeze, the fumes from the cauldron, the sagacious silence of the clock, the unexpected reflection of one of the mirrors - she recalled her youth.

Witches forget their own powers sometimes: when they recall something, there is the risk that that thing will indeed be recalled. Sure enough, there was a soft knock on her door. Standing on the threshold stood precisely what she had recalled: the young girl who had been...herself.

She sort of asked the little girl (though it may have been rhetorical): "What am I to do with you?"

"Oh, I cannot stay, I have so far to go."

"But won't you end up right back here?"

"Yes, but it's too soon."

"Well, be careful. Don't stray. And if you smell gingerbread, run in the other direction."

"I'll take care." With this assurance, the girl turned to leave, but the elder witch called to her.

"Wait." The witch turned from the girl and looked at her little home. She went to the clock and gently put the pendulum in motion. It immediately began its peaceful, patient, arcing swing. If you looked at it upside down, it would look as if it were waving to you, as if it knew that you were leaving.

The witch closed her eyes, made a gesture with her left hand, then did the same with her right hand but the other way, and opened her eyes again.

Moments later, two young girls - one newly young - held hands and walked - then skipped - down the ill-worn path, disappearing into the elongated shadows of the late-summer sun.

The room grew dark. Fire cooled to ash. The mirror had only darkness to reflect. All was still save for the pendulum, left to wave goodbye in its sad, faithful, upside-down way.

The Blue Forest;
or, the Snail and the Number Three
(the real Number Three, not some pretend Number Three)

Once upon a time there was a
river that diminished into a
stream that moderated into a creek that
shrank into a brook that narrowed into a
run that trickled into a small pool in the
middle of The Blue Forest. A blue, Blue

Forest as blue as the cerulean skies of late November afternoons, the air crisp, that once carried the sounds of leaves falling, of twigs cracking, of the fluttering of wings of invisible birds, of whispering, magical bipeds stirring nothing.

The Blue Forest had been quiet for a long time. So very long. The leaves had been falling for eons, it seemed, so graceful and slow they seemed like sere leaves sinking in a jar of clear molasses, floating in some mute medium. A snow globe without snow. And yet the forest would grow still more quiet, until it was absolutely still and absolutely silent. Inertia is a slow process, and inertia was the process that engulfed the blue forest.

The small pool that had very big connections had not known a ripple for so long it took itself for something solid. Its surface was a mirror of blue trees and blue skies, a still life of a frozen forest. Even the wind that traveled quite far to visit became somber, cautious, wary of causing the slightest shudder or vibration. It was positively funereal.

A lot of people and elves come to me and ask, "How did the Blue Forest come to be this way? Some curse? Some heroic failure? A magician imprisoned? A princess under a spell? Some Great Waiting? Is the forest real or some artist's rendering?" I can only sigh and - as if it were a responsibility allotted me from a ship-wrecked spirit - relate what I know. It ain't much, but it may help.

So. Once upon a time there was a river etcetera etcetera a small pool etcetera a mirror of blue trees and blue skies. Around this pool, the Blue Forest, simply loaded with life, natural and magical, though some might say that's redundant. Anyway, teeming and pulsating - as they say - with Life. But then.....

In the Blue Forest lived a snail, one of the creatures least affected by the slow-down. She barely noticed the change except that she suddenly found herself to be the fastest gun in town. She was like a jaguar with a shell on her back: she could outrace anything. Just for fun, she sprinted up and down the length of Carl the snake; for kicks she ran in and out of the yawning jaws of Charlemagne the lion until she grew bored, ran around his face a couple of times, then headed home.

Where was I?

The reason we mention this snail is not for her newfound speed, but because of her part in the whole forest-freeze scenario, for it was she who met the cause of the present state of the Blue Forest, namely the Number Three. Though it really took two for this particular tangle.

Though it is not outrageous that, on a certain day, the Number Three was wending his way through the forest - stranger constructs had wandered there - he was alone, which made him fuzzy. The snail had been masticating on some spongy tree-bark when she looked up and saw the approaching number. Her first thought was that she needed glasses, but the only thing that was out of focus was the number.

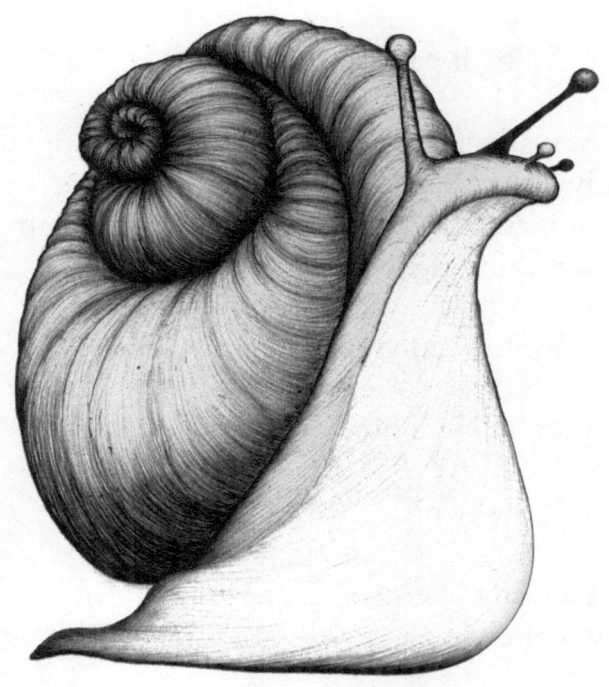

"Hello," said the snail. "Who are you?"

"I'm the number three."

"Three what?"

"Three everything. Like three apples."

"You're three apples?"

"No. I'm the three part of three apples."

"Which part of the apples?"

"Actually, I have nothing to do with apples. I'm a number." (He said this with great emphasis this time, which would clear up everything right away.)

"What can you do?"

"I can tell you how many."

"Like two?"

"Nothing like two!" The Number Three was offended.

"Like four."

"Never!" The Number Three was really offended.

"So only three."

"Yes."

"What if there were only two apples?"

"No. I can't be part of that."

"Because three isn't part of two." (The snail was really trying,)

"Yes."

"What if there were four apples?"

"I can't be part of four either."

"Not even a small part?"

"Not without a vinculum*." (The Number Three was really trying, too.)

"Well, can you show me three without there being three of something?"

"No."

"Can you make something three that isn't three?"

"I guess if you had two other threes, I could be the third three. So there'd be three."

"I...I..."

"One more and you'll have me!" (The number three was actually being sincere.)

The snail was utterly disenchanted. She said, "I may be wrong, but I'm pretty sure you are the most useless thing I have ever come across. And you hurt my eyes."

"Only because I'm not connected to anything."

The snail huffed, bid the Number Three good day, and slid off.

Well, as the saying goes, you never know. It turned out that the Number Three had a close personal acquaintance with the whole gang of counting numbers, almost every whole number, and a mob of integers who had no little influence in the field of, say, everything.

He told them of his exchange with the snail of the Blue Forest and, to a number, they decided to boycott the Forest.

Without numbers, no counting; no counting, no time; no time, no change; no change…no change. Hence, the Blue Forest's full throttle approach to a full stop.

Some time later - though for obvious reasons, we don't know how much time later - a firefly arrived who gave a cogent argument that time was arbitrary and that change was independent of such silly inventions as numbers. He knew for a fact that stuff was going on way before numbers came along, lots of stuff. Important stuff. This point was so irrefutable that in no time - and that is entirely accurate - the Blue Forest was chugging along again like nothing had happened. Which really hadn't.

The end.

N.B. *For our purposes, a vinculum is the line that separates the numerator from the denominator in a fraction.

Horace The Frog
Seeks A Story

There was once a frog who hadn't always been a frog named Horace who felt he needed a story. That's a bit confusing. He had always been named Horace; that isn't what changed. He was not always a frog. That's what I mean. Anyway, syntax.

Because he felt he needed a story, he went searching for one. One would think with so many of them floating around, drifting here and there, hiding in swamps and behind tree trunks, sleeping in branches, galloping beside knights errant, pining away in castle towers or sighing significantly in dark dungeons, hitching rides on the backs of bluebirds and witches, sitting in circles around camp fires, or in half-circles around hearths with black cauldrons hanging over logs and branches and fast-firing autumn leaves, or making tracks on vague paths leading somewhere or nowhere, stories would be easy to find. Horace would say to himself, "It's not like I'm seeking an anthology. I just need one. Don't ask me why. I don't know. I just feel that I should have one. Everyone else does. I mean, really, everything else in this crazy forest has a story. Stop and ask a rock or a blade of grass or a lichen." Though he did say this, for the sake of complete transparency,

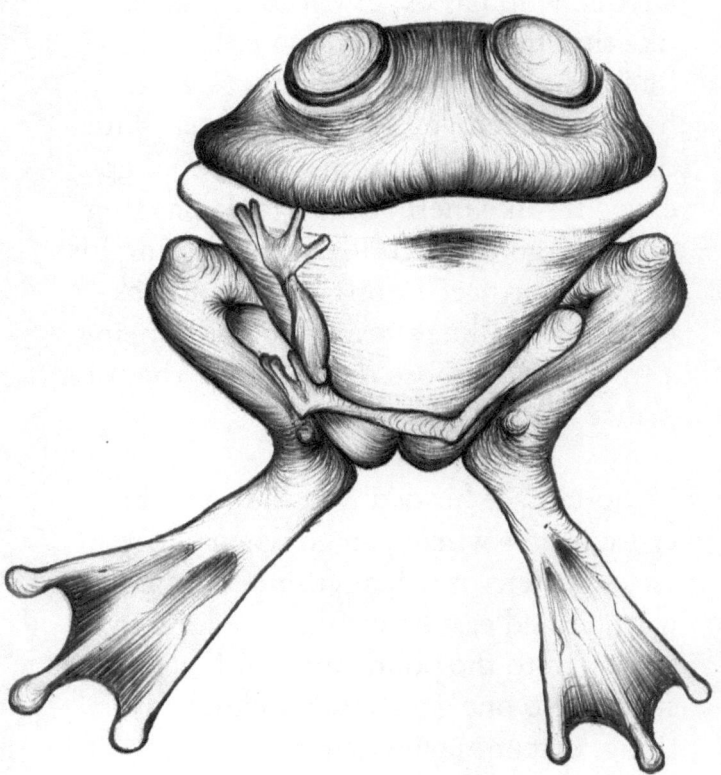

Horace did not know then nor does he know now exactly what lichen is. Not even approximately.

You would think that a frog named Horace who had not always been a frog would not be in need of a story. Not that the name matters, but you get the point: anyone who has experienced a change like that must have a tale to tell. Unless he forgot his story. Maybe that's what happens when you go through that kind of thing: you have to forget or you'll go crazy. It's like mercy amnesia. What frog wants to go through life remembering his days as a prince? I don't have that backwards: if you knew anything about being a frog, you'd choose that life over that of a prince any day.

So Horace headed west, not only because west is where you go when you're seeking pretty much anything, but because if he headed east he would have hit a tree; north led to the pond; and south was just stupid. No one goes south seeking anything, except maybe retirement.

Behind him, the sun nudged him along; before him, his shadow - understandably not much of a shadow - led the way. Post-meridian, the sun would slow him, get in his eyes, and his shadow would trail behind. But the desire for a story was powerful enough to keep him pushing on.

Eventually, Horace came upon a magazine rack - if that isn't too implausible in a story about a frog from a magic forest - and he came to a halt. He had never seen one before, so he could not help but be impressed by this edifice of glossy paper and sculpted metal. Do we not all feel this sensation when we see that irresistible wall of printed riches?

Horace, enchanted by those froth-inducing photographs and captions, pored through them all, scrutinizing every image and syllable.

Exactly twenty magazines later, Horace headed east. And they say you can't find wisdom in those types of publication!

The Aardvark and The Seamstress

Once upon a time there was a little aardvark that really had it made. (By little I'm speaking from the aardvarkian perspective; roughly 24 kilograms.) Days of dozing under a damp, rotting tree trunk; nights of roaming through a forest loaded with big fat juicy ants and no predators whatsoever to lose sleep over. A life of undisturbed luxury: oh, what did he do to deserve such a blessed existence? Who could not envy the pig with the toothy proboscis?

Then there was the other eponymous character. A little woman of the ruddy-cheeked, rotund, rocking-chair variety who wore calico and a little white apron, with her white hair tied back in a bun. Just as sweet and adorable as could be.

How could the paths of these two possibly cross in a meaningful way? Well, the aardvark occasionally traveled through her little garden of flowers or her little garden of vegetables, and once in a while parked himself under her porch and snoozed. She may notice. She may even care. But not so much that she would drop a stitch over it.

Now this woman was a seamstress of no mean skills. She could use a sewing needle, knitting needle, crocheting needle, darning needle, Cleopatra's needle, Chinese needle, leprechaun's needle, S-shaped needle, C-shaped needle, harness needle, devil's needle, carpenter's needle, flogspotter's needle, Estonian needle, crimp needle, pentacore needle, Fluellen needle, widdny needle, Offerhuasen needle, Potsville-Haurmann Grasping needle, torch needle, asterhex needle, Donnelly crafting needle, curved semper-drifting hasp-and-clutch needle, Forsaw-Verklempten needle, fine draper's needle, alteration needle, finishing needle, Smith-and-Warner's tapered needle (style 6c, winter catalogue), parson's needle....you get the drift: the woman was a pro. She could create a pair of stockings while eating a grape; she could give you the Bayeux tapestry in a short week.

Rumor has it she created such a realistic rendering of the magic forest, you couldn't tell it from the real thing. There was a certain prince who made a wrong turn somewhere, ended up in her hand-stitched enchanted land and spent two years wandering around before he realized his mistake. If he had not gotten his sword stuck in a tiny stitch - almost unraveling the Red Dragon and part of the ominous sky behind him - he'd still be there.

After the prince exited, the seamstress fixed it up in a jiffy. You would need a magnifying glass to detect the tiny scarlet scar on the dragon's ear, the result of a variation in thread color that was entirely the manufacturer's fault. How many times do we have to suffer - and suffer from - these lapses in quality control? On the other hand, when you're ordering spools of thread by the gross, you have to figure a faded bit of red once in a blue.

How did we get here?

One day - ah, here we go - one day the aardvark was sleeping under the porch of the seamstress, nestled into the cool earth, when she - the seamstress - startled by a starling flying right past her ear, dropped her needle. The needle fell right between two floorboards and landed on - in - the neck of the snoozing creature.

The pinch of the needle made his big, leathery ears twitch; the twitch in turn dislodged the needle, which then fell sideways onto his neck. (A detail that better be made relevant very soon if it is to be justified.)

The needle had a lovely yellow thread in it; this thread now ran from the spool on the seamstress' lap through the porch and was now latched onto the aardvark.

Okay, it wasn't yellow; it was gold. In fact, it was the legendary Golden Thread of The Gallant Giant. (The name was entirely deserved.) This thread would animate whatever it became part of; a golden cloud or sunbeam; a bell or bird; the golden equipage of a horse.

There was a lot of this magic in her work. The student of her tapestries would first see a spark, a seeming trick of the eye; then another trick: did that horse raise its leg? Had the shadow of that tree shifted? Did the stem of that pear look different? Was that ripple in the stream always there? Did that girl lower her pail a bit deeper into the water?

Then the motions seemed to be more pronounced; they seemed to match the movements of the outside world. It was lovely. Skill is one thing, but the right material surely helps. Luckily, the seamstress didn't have to use it sparingly; the giant had given her hanks, skeins, parcels, leas, mommes, bundles - whichever way it's measured - of it. (This is where the stuff comes from; thank goodness it comes from somewhere.)

The seamstress pulled on the thread but it wasn't coming up through the little divide; all that pulling was merely causing the needle to dance around and tickle the aardvark's neck. He grunted and awoke or the other way around. Either way, he wasn't thrilled.

Perhaps it was because he was still a bit woozy from his sleep or perhaps because of his lousy eyesight, he mistook the dancing needle for an ant.

The rest of the story is history, but I have no idea what it is.

The Knight's Story

Surviving fragments of
The Knight and His Shadow Companion

"All existence is hypothetical
until it meets a sword."
(Viletius Honorus Lucubrius)

And, as his strength
Failed him at length,
He met a pilgrim shadow -
"Shadow," said he,
"Where can it be -
This land of Eldorado?"

Over the mountains
Of the Moon,
Down the Valley of the Shadow,
Ride, boldly ride,"
The shade replied -
If you seek for Eldorado!

(from *Eldorado,* Edgar Allen Poe)

Once upon a time, there was a spoiled little princess who was raised on buttermilk poured from pitchers of gold. She slept on the most obliging of mattresses; she walked a path pillowed with goose-down and servants; her retinue was gloriously obedient to her every whim; and her every whim was as dull as a scullery maid's apron. She grew to be the White Queen. Her kingdom, her chessboard; her subjects, her pieces: she would move them or topple them as she pleased.

And that's all you have to know about the princess.

[The Talking Forest .]

The verdant forest echoed with the susurrations of the trees, each whispering an ancient admonition into the ears of our knight. The words began in their trunks, vibrating to an internal sound; they would rise - those words - to the branches, which would shake, then to the leaves that would fan them - these words - to the passing knight.

"In fleeing the ashes, fear perishes in the coals."

"Any excuse will serve a tyrant."

"Only cowards insult dying majesty."

"The city is the teacher of the man."

"Longer than deeds liveth the word."

"The song precedes the singer."

"To foolish men belongeth a love for things afar."

"….a man hath no morrow.."

"Makers of bows best know the bough."

"Gold is best used to choke a dragon; second best, to choke a man."

"No evil can befall a good man, either in life or in death."

"That which is found in the refrain is lost on the spit."

"Oh, to be a Frog...."

"...sing them, I pray you."

"The wolf is envy and hath woman's eyes."

"It is enough to have perished once."

"Blossoming Spring is Death's most evil emissary."

"We desire nothing so much as what we ought not to have."

"Here is Death, twitching my ear: 'Live, says he, for I am coming.'"

"It is not every question that deserves an answer."

"Be not inundated, though the flood of days be imminent."

"Not lost…"

"…nor can the willow beg."

"…as it is it shall be."

"Alexander wept…"

"Travel the exile's path."

"…fate is relentless"

"Hooded and bowed, his shuffle shifts the stones, his road."

"…the soul of this world."

"The blow fallen no grieving can amend."

"…should I be fit?"

Said the knight, "These things surely come from the elder gods." His shadow concurred.

"Do you exist always, even in darkness?"

"Is existence determined by visibility?"

Even great and noble knights grow weary sometimes of the quest, persevering through strange lands near and far. There were hours when he would fall asleep inside his golden suit, less smooth and lustrous than it had been before the dust and wind and rain, the clashes with sword, adaga, ax, bludgeon, assegai, the arrows of long bow and cross bow, pike, thunderbolt, spear of ice, spear of rock, dagger, cutlass, dirk, poniard, falchion, glaive, foil, shield and mace and lance, the smoke and fire of dragons, rocks and boulders hurled by giants, hellions, trolls and other miscreations, the scratches and dents from the claws of lions and griffins, the spells of witches, fairies and elves, and the ardent piercing shafts from the battered fortresses forged from the embittered hearts of love-warped women.

[(fragment from) Chapter the Next]

One night, as the winds blew furiously and the sky threatened torrents, the knight came upon a woman, bent low, cupping water from a pond. Her frame was so slight she was almost lost in the folds of her heavy cloak and the heavier rain; her hood covered her head almost entirely. At the sound of his approach, she almost sank into the wet ground. The knight dismounted to offer help.

"Why do you hide yourself, maiden?"

She turned her head up and pulled back her hood. Her face was spectral and grotesque; the individual features seemed not to fit, as if her face were a composite of many faces, assembled, as it were, from parts not of the original.

"How so?" he asked in a whisper.

"I am a woman warped by envy. I despised my own appearance, wishing for this girl's hair, that maiden's eyes, that woman's nose... My wishes were granted."

She explained that she grew more hideous as her parts grew and changed, as if each part held its own destiny. One leg grew fat, the other remained thin. Her left hand grew gnarled and stiff, her fingers like branches of an ancient tree; the right hand became palsied and shook violently. Her mouth was too small for her face; her eyes too large, as if her features had been drawn on a balloon before it became fully inflated.

She called the knight to see her reflection in the pool. The image was lovely.

"This is you?"

"Was. This is as I looked before ever I received my wish." A tear fell into the pond, disturbing the image in the water.

"So you had your wish."

She smiled.

"Can this spell be undone?" he asked.

"I do not know."

"Who would know?"

"The Dam of Basilshire. She who granted my wish."

"We shall find her."

[The Last Extant Fragment]

"Very well, child, what is your wish?" asked the witch.

"I wish to look as I did…as was intended, before I was touched by your spell."

The witch went to the hearth and reached confidently into the fire. With her leathery fingers she pulled out a few sticks of burning straw. She then took her other hand and held it over the flame, uttering an incantation.

The knight saw the young woman swoon, then miraculously revert to the image the knight has seen in the water, then suddenly change into a robin, flutter around the witch's hut and fly out of the window.

The witch saw the knight's expression.

"Thus she was before the spell. A robin chick too young to care for herself, separated from her mother. I adopted her and gave her human form. Whenever I give creatures human form, they develop human frailties. Hers was envy, despite her beauty. The spell I put on her was a lesson, never intended to be permanent. She is free now. She will be fine.

"Sir knight, if it would not displease you, dine with me tonight before you continue your journey."

Beneath the moon, the knight dreamt that he was being guided by a palpable though invisible hand. And words were spoken to him as they were in the Talking Forest, though he could not determine from whence they came.

"What you seek is often too close to be seen."

"The light is not always the good, nor the dark always bad."

"The easy road is not the right road."

"Never fight the lesser foe."

"Futility is a man who clutches a crown."

"Time erases all."

When the sun rose, the knight saw the witch again stirring her cauldron. He bade her direct him.

"Your quest is ended."

"How so?"

"You have reached the end of your

time. You are an aged man, too old to go on from here."

The knight laughed at her. "Too old? Nay, I have many strong years before me."

"Behold," said the witch, holding a mirror before the knight. Aghast, he tentatively, disbelievingly touched his crooked, wrinkled fingers to his withered face. It was as if he were putting his fingers into a flame. His hair was thin and grey, his beard mere wisps dangling from his chin.

"How so?"

"You have slept a long time, my son. Forty years to the day."

"Not so!" He stood up and suddenly felt gravity press him down to the bench. He again looked at what was now his hand. He could neither fully close nor fully straighten it. He turned it over and back, studying the blue veins and colorations. He marveled. Then he rested his head in those hands and closed his eyes.

"Is this a spell? My time…can I….can it be retrieved?"

"Dear, foolish one, you spent your life to find your life. Wasted time to find time. Now you know. You are less a knight than a fool, though you were a noble knight, indeed.

"There is hope. You will follow the road to its own end; pray you reach it before you reach your own. There you will find your grail. Thou art worthy of glory, though thou shalt not have it. Not in the time in which we reside, but there will be a time for you."

The ancient knight rose and turned to the door, where the sun stretched shadows. He thought of his own and he hastened as quickly as he could to meet his fellow traveler. Would he, too, be different?

Indeed his shadow was. He was smaller, frail and bent. The knight looked at the armor tied to the back of a nag that was not the same horse upon which he had arrived.

"Shadow, has it been forty years?"

"I have waited as long."

"You are loyal. What do you think of this? Do we move on?"

"What choice? To linger here will be our death."

"And to move on?

"The road shall be harder from now on. Our pace shall be slow."

Echoed the knight: "Our pace shall be slow. And we shall feel the warmth of the sun. And we shall feel the bitter, bracing icy rain on our face. And we shall feel every bump and rock on the road. And our back shall bend and our vision fail. And we shall know all before us anew. This is our journey. And when we rest, we shall rest at our choosing. Could one ask for a better life?"

The knight mounted his horse and shook the reins.

(And here the story ends.)

The Hermit and The Queen

" Dec: 31. (Sun.) (1871).
Nearly midnight. The past
year has made little
change in the position
of myself, or the family..."
(Lewis Caroll, Diary entry)

Once upon a time there was a
hermit who lived in a hidden part of the
magical forest. There was barely a discernible path to his little cabin. It was so sound-
less, the surrounding flora and fauna felt it a
matter of respect to remain as quiet as they
could be, as if the area were a cloister or
sanctuary. The soundlessness enhanced the
colors of daisies and daffodils, the smell of
moss, the movements of growth and decay,
the taste of Time aged in oak.

The hermit had once been a knight.
If you saw him without that beard, you'd
swear you had seen him somewhere before.
He looked awfully familiar.

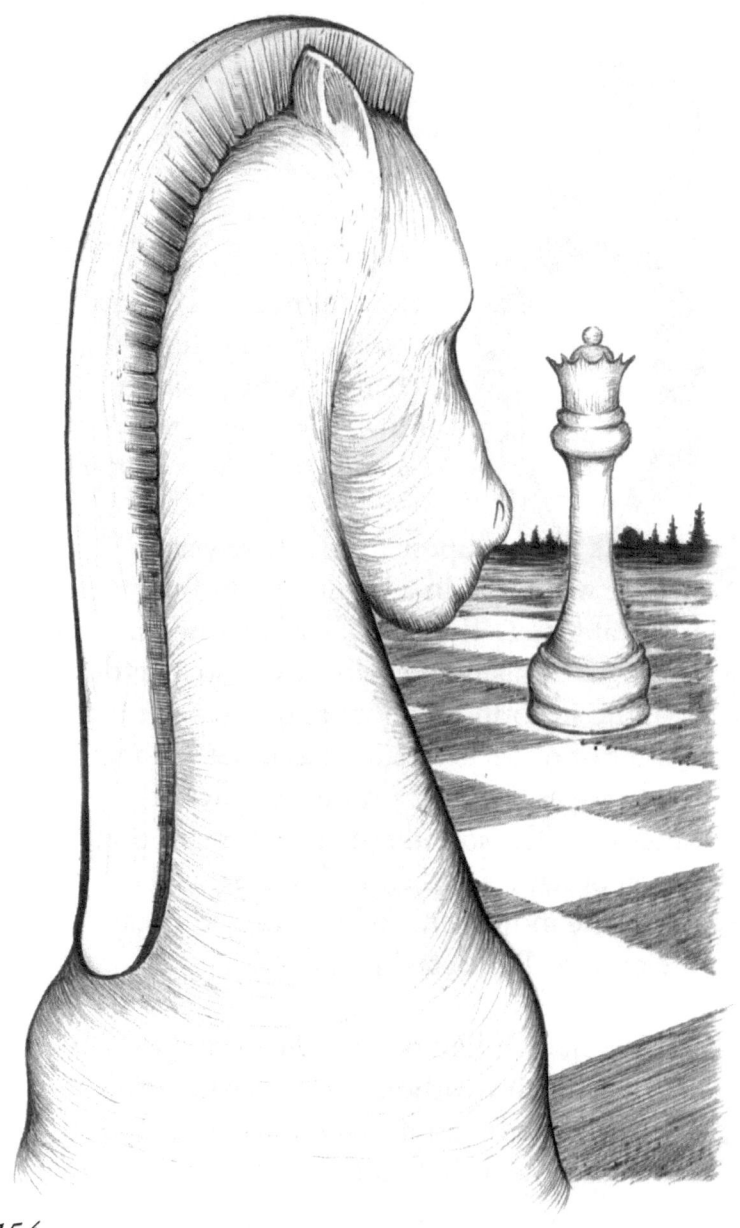

His shadow (His shadow! Of cours
shared the knight's secluded existence,
which had gone on for many tranquil yea

One day, when he was returning from a
brook where he had been helping a family
of badgers build a dam, he saw a mottled
horse standing near his home. It was one of
those brilliantly conceived horses that was

k with white mark-
k markings. But
olute in their per-
blackness, the
the other. They
noon on a clear, frigid
ne shadow loved this analogy
ncle in the heart of a shadow.

Then he saw - oh, wonders! - The
White Queen. She sat on a tree stump,
her back straight, her left hand resting
atop her right, both resting on her lap.
She wore, of course, white gloves, a white
gown, and white boots. Nothing would
dare sully her, not a mote of dust, not an
ort of food, not the tiniest drop of dew:
she was one of those few creatures that
nature would not touch in deference to
her sublimity.

Her hair was white and in it a bejeweled diadem that seemed to collect and
diffuse light, creating a nimbus around
her. She was much older than she had
been when he last saw her.

She spoke as if she were continuing a conversation begun long ago. "The moves on my chessboard are without limit. But the board itself is fixed: sixty-four perfect alternating squares, no matter which piece stands where....(Did she sigh here?)...all these positions, all their variety...seemed not to matter anymore; it was the board that I saw, only those squares squared, only the fixed quadrate forms locked into each other.... (Another sigh?)"

Who cannot appreciate when a queen uses the word quadrate?

The former knight could not help admiring her. Her straight hair, her straight spine, her straight speech: the personification of some celestial geometry, created by compass and protractor. And some divine hand.

Perhaps it was the return of an old habit, but he felt the urge to kneel before her. His right hand instinctively reached to his side to sweep back his scabbard; he smiled at his forgetfulness: that impediment to genuflection had been abandoned long ago.

He lowered his head. He was not sure if he should look into her eyes. Indeed, when their eyes did meet, he averted his gaze, typically choosing to study something at his feet.

"How did you find me?"

"The board does not end at the edges of my kingdom. It is less discernible, but it continues. And moves are always moves."

"Why did you seek me?"

"To bring you back."

The knight tried to look at her, but her beauty got in the way. His heart, which had been content, now knew something else. The beat of his heart seemed to be heard all around him. Little ears pricked up all over the place.

"Dear knight, you must return with me. As it should be."

Even the wind paused to hear what the knight would decide.

Dear Reader, if you wish to know what our dear knight - and, yes, his loyal shadow - chose, merely look at your chessboard. There you will see the White Queen standing proudly among her retinue, and right beside her the most loyal and handsome of knights. He would live and die for her a thousand times. As it should be, forever and ever.

The End

Postscript

I met Biff Wellington at the All-In Truck Stop outside of Las Vegas a few years ago. The All-In is on 95, just before it hooks north. Around there are Summerlin, Angel Park, Lone Mountain, Adderton, and a town called Extra Parts. Extra Parts, Nevada. I've been there.

Inside, the quality of the food was determined by mass, volume and ketchup. Outside, forty pumps under a football-field-size scaffold that held a thousand florescent tubes, half of them dead, the other half, half dead. From a very great distance, it appeared to be a glowing oasis. That tells you what distance can do.

And this oasis was peopled by all sorts of tribe-less nomads who zig-zagged without reason or plan, their paths as absurd as those of moths or mosquitoes, flying and flitting and sometimes meeting briefly, briefly.

And during those night-less nights,
around the forty diesel-fuel pumps
danced the local dryads: hookers and drug
dealers. For obvious reasons, amphet-
amines were popular. Cocaine. Rarely,
someone would drop coins in the slots, of
which there were five.

I was at a booth inside the diner. As
always, it was two in the morning. The ten
other patrons were as red-eyed and worn
as I was. We all had too much road in us.
Funny: you're always supposed to be somewhere you're not: Strongbow, Tennessee;
Slingshot, Arkansas; Truth, Texas; Song of
Christ, North Dakota. The place you're
supposed to be, that's where you spend
almost no time. You live where you drive.
It's all backwards.

Anyway, in walks what ends up being Biff Wellington, himself. But at that time he was nobody number 11 at the All-In Truck Stop on 95.

No one makes it a habit to socialize in these places, but this guy sat down opposite me in my booth. He didn't look at me right away, but waved over the waitress and ordered steak and eggs and coffee and a coke. Then he leaned back and breathed. Then he looked at me.

"Where you from?" he asked, then added, "It don't matter. I went to school for a while. That don't matter, either. I left to make a living. Man, I'm tired."

I saw this guy didn't want to hear things; when you know you've got nothing to add, you should just shut up. Some people don't get that.

The waitress brought his coffee. He asked her if he could borrow her pen.

He took out from his jacket a packet of papers that looked like they'd been used to herd bison or to clean windshields: rolled, wrinkled, stained and damp.

He dropped the bundle on the table and wrote on the top page: "Good luck. I been carrying you long enough. You're on your own. Bifford C. Wellington." Then his food came and he ate. At one point, he took his fork and used it to nudge the packet towards me.

"I'm going off the road for a while. I meant to do something with this. I meant to do something with a lot of things. This road, it ain't so good for getting things done."

We both sighed at that. "Yep,' he said.

"Well," he said. "That's about it." He looked me in the eye and he shook my hand. He dropped money on the table and walked out and that was that.

I asked the waitress for a plastic bag;
I didn't want the bundle to get any more
raggedy than it was. I felt it was something. To tell the truth, I felt for the first
time that something was something. That's
the only way I can put it.

So, if you have any questions, I'm defi-
nitely the wrong guy. I could have said that
to Biff Wellington: "You got the wrong
guy." Maybe I wasn't. Maybe he knew better than I did.

Anyway, that's the story. Just remember: the guy you really want to talk to is
Biff Wellington.

One more thing: he was a couple of
coins short when the check came, but by
then he was gone gone gone. But that's
okay. It makes the story better.

—TAYoung